W9-BXX-308

Herbster Readers

THE WINNING BASKET

Written by Cecilia Minden and Joanne Meier • Illustrated by Bob Ostrom
Created by Herbie J. Thorpe

The Child's World

ABOUT THE AUTHORS

Cecilia Minden, PhD, is the former director of the Language and Literacy Program at the Harvard Graduate School of Education. She is now a reading consultant for school and library publications. She earned her PhD in reading education from the University of Virginia. Cecilia and her husband, Dave Cupp, live outside Chapel Hill, North Carolina. They enjoy sharing their love of reading with their grandchildren, Chelsea and Qadir.

Joanne Meier, PhD, has worked as an elementary school teacher, university professor, and researcher. She earned her BA in early childhood education from the University of South Carolina, and her MEd and PhD in education from the University of Virginia. She currently works as a literacy consultant for schools and private organizations. Joanne lives in Virginia with her husband Eric, daughters Kella and Erin, two cats, and a gerbil.

ABOUT THE ILLUSTRATOR

Bob Ostrom has been illustrating children's books for nearly twenty years. A graduate of the New England School of Art & Design at Suffolk University, Bob has worked for such companies as Disney, Nickelodeon, and Cartoon Network. He lives in North Carolina with his wife Melissa and three children, Will, Charlie, and Mae.

ABOUT THE SERIES CREATOR

Herbie J. Thorpe had long envisioned a beginning-readers' series about a fun, energetic bear with a big imagination. Herbie is a book lover and an avid supporter of libraries and the role they play in fostering the love of reading. He consults with librarians and matches them with the perfect books for their students and patrons. He lives in Louisiana with his wife Misty and their daughter Carson.

Published in the United States of America by The Child's World®
1980 Lookout Drive • Mankato, MN 56003-1705
800-599-READ • www.childsworld.com

Acknowledgments
The Child's World®: Mary Berendes, Publishing Director
The Design Lab: Kathleen Petelinsek, Design;
Gregory Lindholm, Page Production
Assistant colorist: Richard Carbajal

Library of Congress Cataloging-in-Publication Data
 Minden, Cecilia.
  The winning basket / written by Cecilia Minden and Joanne
Meier ; illustrated by Bob Ostrom.
    p. cm. — (Herbster readers)
  Summary: "In this simple story belonging to the third level of
Herbster Readers, young Herbie's imagination is sparked by a
classroom visit from his favorite pro basketball player"—Provided
by publisher.
  ISBN 978-1-60253-019-5 (library bound : alk. paper)
 [1. Basketball—Fiction. 2. Imagination—Fiction. 3. Bears— Fiction.]
I. Meier, Joanne D. II. Ostrom, Bob, ill. III. Title. IV. Series.
 PZ7.M6539Wi 2008
 [E]—dc22   2008002598

Herbie Bear's class was
expecting a surprise visitor.

"Who could it be?" asked Herbie.

"Maybe it's Chelsea Cat, the famous singer," said Kim.

"Maybe it's J. Q. Blue, the superhero," said Michael.

8

A tall figure stepped into the room.

"Class, please say hello to my brother, David," said Mr. Stone.

Herbie couldn't believe it!

Mr. Stone's brother was 3-Point Stone!

3-Point played for Herbie's favorite basketball team, the Wildcats.

The class gave 3-Point their full attention.

Everyone, that is, except Herbie.

Herbie was already on the
Wildcats' home court.

It was the play-off game
against the Black Knights.

17

Herbie and 3-Point ran down the court.

They dribbled, they passed, and they shot!

The Wildcats scored. The Knights scored. The game was tied!

It was the final seconds of the game.
Herbie passed the ball to 3-Point.

3-Point tried to make the shot. No luck!
He passed the ball back to Herbie.

Herbie ran to do a layup.

Slam dunk! He scored! The Wildcats won!

The crowd went wild.
"Herbie! Herbie!" they shouted.

"Herbie? Herbie?" said Mr. Stone.

"Would you like to meet my brother David?"

Herbie went over by the other students.

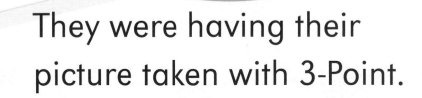

They were having their
picture taken with 3-Point.

"I've heard a lot about you, Herbie," said 3-Point.

"Maybe someday we can play basketball together."

Herbie just smiled.